Katy Duck,
Flower Girl

By Alyssa Satin Capucilli Illustrated by Henry Cole

Ready-to-Read

Simon Spotlight

New York   London   Toronto   Sydney   New Delhi

For Dave and Kristin, *Tanti auguri*, always . . .
—A. S. C.

SIMON SPOTLIGHT
An imprint of Simon & Schuster Children's Publishing Division
1230 Avenue of the Americas, New York, New York 10020
Text copyright © 2013 by Alyssa Satin Capucilli
Illustrations copyright © 2013 by Henry Cole
SIMON SPOTLIGHT, READY-TO-READ, and colophon are registered trademarks of
Simon & Schuster, Inc.
For information about special discounts for bulk purchases, please contact Simon & Schuster
Special Sales at 1-866-506-1949 or business@simonandschuster.com.
The Simon & Schuster Speakers Bureau can bring authors to your live event. For more information or
to book an event contact the Simon & Schuster Speakers Bureau at 1-866-248-3049 or visit our website
at www.simonspeakers.com.
Manufactured in the United States of America 0413 LAK
First Edition
10 9 8 7 6 5 4 3 2 1
Library of Congress Cataloging-in-Publication Data
Capucilli, Alyssa Satin.
Katy Duck, flower girl / by Alyssa Satin Capucilli ; illustrated by Henry Cole.— 1st ed.
p. cm. — (Ready-to-read)
Summary: When Katy learns that she will be the flower girl at her Aunt Ella's wedding, she begins to
practice swaying like a daffodil in the breeze and stretching like a tulip in the sun.
ISBN 978-1-4424-7278-5 (pbk.) — ISBN 978-1-4424-7279-2 (hardcover) — ISBN 978-1-4424-7280-8
(ebook) — [1. Flower girls—Fiction. 2. Weddings—Fiction.
3. Ducks—Fiction.] I. Cole, Henry, 1955- ill. II. Title.
PZ7.C179Kf 2013
[E]—dc23
2012016455

"I have wonderful news,"
Mrs. Duck told Katy Duck.
"Aunt Ella is getting
married!"

"At the wedding, Emmett
will carry the rings. You
will be the flower girl,
Katy," said Mrs. Duck.

"Tra-la-la. Quack! Quack!"
A wedding? A flower girl?
Katy Duck was so excited!

"I must practice,"
said Katy.
Outside, Katy Duck
swayed like a daffodil
in the breeze.

She stretched like a
tulip in the sun.
She could hardly wait
to be a flower girl.

At last, it was time
for the wedding.

"Come along, Katy,"
said Mrs. Duck.
"We must get ready."

First, Mrs. Duck
dressed Emmett.
Katy thought he looked
a bit like Mr. Duck.

Then Mrs. Duck
helped Aunt Ella.
Katy had never seen
anyone so beautiful!

"Now it is your turn, Katy,"
said Mrs. Duck.

Katy Duck closed her eyes.
She took a deep breath.

"Tra-la-la. Oh no!"
cried Katy Duck.
"That dress does not
look like a flower at all."

"Oh, Katy," said Mrs. Duck.
"A flower girl does not
look like a flower."

"A flower girl **tosses**
flowers at a wedding!"
said Mrs. Duck.
Katy looked down.

"But maybe **this** flower girl can dance like a flower too!" Aunt Ella said. Now Katy smiled.

The music began.
Emmett carried the rings
very carefully.
He looked proud!

"You're next, Katy,"
Aunt Ella said
with a smile.
She gave Katy a big hug.

Katy tossed
flower petals
to her left.

She tossed
them to her right.

And as the music soared,
Katy Duck swayed
like a daffodil and
stretched like a tulip.

Everyone agreed she was
a wonderful flower girl.

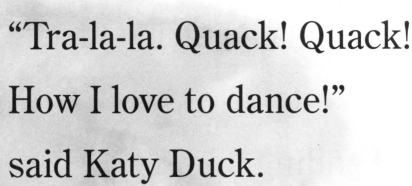

"Tra-la-la. Quack! Quack!
How I love to dance!"
said Katy Duck.

"Tra-la-la. Quack! Quack!
How I do love
a wedding, too!"